STEPHEN'S FROG

Barbara Feldman

Annick Press Ltd. • Toronto, Canada

For The Boys

Annick Press Ltd.

Annick Press gratefully acknowledges the support of the Canada Council and the Ontario Arts Council.

Canadian Cataloguing in Publication Data

Feldman, Barbara, 1949–
   Stephens' frog

(Annick toddler series)
ISBN 1-55037-200-9 (bound) ISBN 1-55037-201-7 (pbk.)

1. Stories without words.   I. Title.   II. Series.

PS8561.E53S7   1991   jC813′.54   C91-094245-5
PZ7.F45St   1991

The art in this book was rendered in fabric appliqué. The text has been set in Garamond by Attic Typesetting.

Distributed in Canada and the USA by:
Firefly Books Ltd.
250 Sparks Avenue
Willowdale, Ontario   M2H 2S4

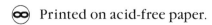 Printed on acid-free paper.

Printed and bound in Canada by
D.W. Friesen and Sons, Altona, Manitoba